Jonny

D1461228

Go to www.maxflash.co.uk
and enter this code:
JH30PS11LB29
for your ... ies, downloads
and ...

STRIPES PUBLISHING
An imprint of Magi Publications
1 The Coda Centre, 189 Munster Road, London SW6 6AW

A paperback original
First published in Great Britain in 2009

Text copyright © Jonny Zucker, 2009
Illustrations copyright © Ned Woodman, 2009

ISBN: 978-1-84715-093-6

Printed and bound in the UK.

2 4 6 8 10 9 7 5 3 1

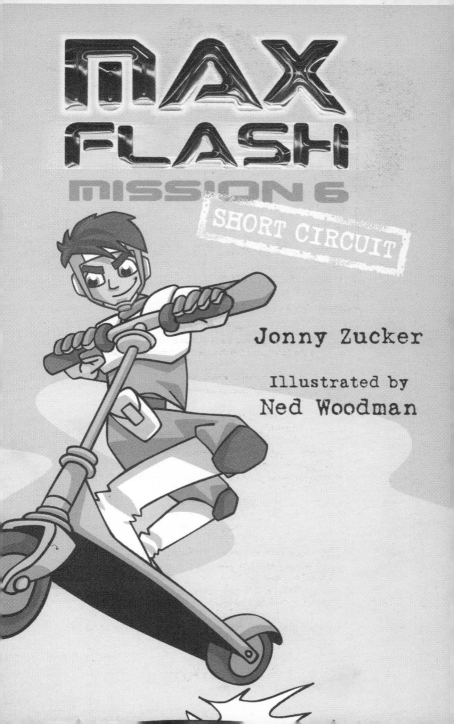

MAX FLASH
MISSION 6
SHORT CIRCUIT

Jonny Zucker

Illustrated by
Ned Woodman

MISSION 6

CHAPTER 1

Max Flash was trapped. Only his head and feet
stuck out from the metal box, and he was
blinded by the bright lights shining from the
ceiling. His body was tensed for action. He
heard the sound of whispered voices and
twisted to the right just as a huge steel saw
sliced through the case, narrowly missing his
arm. It lodged into a slot on the opposite side
and stayed firmly in place. Max twisted again
as a second saw pierced the case, this one only
just missing his leg.

A line of sweat trickled down his forehead. He knew that timing and body position were everything in this situation; one false move and he'd be sushi.

Saw after saw followed, and Max dodged them by rapid twists and turns of his body. He was twisted to the limit now, every joint feeling the strain of holding its position. One more saw and he'd be finished.

But instead of another flash of metal piercing the case, Max watched with relief as the first of the saws was whipped out of the box. The others followed in quick succession. Slowly he straightened his body. He pushed up with his arms and the lid of the case sprung open. He sat up triumphantly and waved his arms in the air.

The crowd went wild, cheering and clapping. Max acknowledged their applause and leaped down on to the stage. The audience rose to their feet, their catcalls and shouts rising.

His mum and dad strode across the stage to join him. Then the three of them took a bow.

As the heavy stage curtain fell, Dad put an arm round Max's shoulder.

"You were brilliant," he said proudly.

"As always," added Mum.

"Don't embarrass me!" groaned Max.

"Come on," said Dad, "get changed as quickly as possible. It's a school night. Let's get you home."

Max's parents, Montgomery and Carly Flash (stage names – The Great Montello and Mystical Cariba) were magicians. Max had been taking part in their shows for some time now and his favourite part of the show was definitely the grand finale – *The Saws of Death*.

Max was allowed to do several performances a month, so long as he kept up with his schoolwork. He loved being onstage, but keeping up with his schoolwork wasn't quite as much fun.

MAX FLASH

As the audience filed out of the theatre, Max's parents went to their changing room and Max went to his. That's what he liked best about performing at the Royal Theatre in London – he got a room all to himself! He shut the door and sat down at his dressing table. He was busy reliving the performance in his head, when he was surprised to see his reflection vanish from the mirror. A second later the cold, blue-eyed face of Zavonne appeared in its place.

"Max," she said seriously, "I have something urgent to discuss with you."

MAX FLASH MISSION 6

CHAPTER 2

Max knew by now that he shouldn't be surprised when Zavonne's image appeared in the most unexpected places, but it still freaked him out.

She can get anywhere!

Zavonne worked for an organization called the DFEA (the Department for Extraordinary Activity). The DFEA dealt with strange and inexplicable events. If a gang of Zorcan Vultures from the planet Proog were heading to earth, the DFEA would cut them off. If plague-bearing

Stone Demons began emerging from the world's chalk quarries, the DFEA would move in to repel them. And they dealt with all these perilous situations before the official authorities were even aware there was a problem.

Max had been recruited as a DFEA Operative because of his incredible contortionist powers and his mastery of magic – skills he'd honed by performing in his parents' shows. His mum and dad had carried out a couple of DFEA missions in the past too – that's how the organization had come to hear about Max – but that was way back. Max had now carried out *five* DFEA missions single-handed.

"For the last twenty-four hours," said Zavonne, "the DFEA has been picking up bursts of strange magnetic waves from a warehouse by the river Thames in London."

Zavonne's face vanished from the mirror and an image of a huge steel warehouse appeared.

"We staked out the building," Zavonne's

voice continued over the image, "and after one of these wave transmissions, we spotted these two interesting-looking characters."

Max watched as two figures emerged from the warehouse. One was about six feet tall, the other no more than four and a half feet.

They were both wearing motorbike gear – black leather jackets and trousers, and heavy black biking boots. Underneath their crash helmets their faces were covered with silver balaclavas. They mounted a large motorbike and sped away from the warehouse.

"A DFEA team tracked them and watched them visiting a range of locations," said Zavonne. "At each one they stopped to take photos."

The image quickly cut to footage of the two figures posing for each other on a busy shopping street in London, followed by them standing in front of a large cinema in Leicester Square – both popular tourist destinations.

Isn't Zavonne being a bit ... paranoid?

"Surely there's nothing wrong with having your photo taken," said Max, "even if you are wearing a balaclava and have come from a warehouse that's sending out magnetic waves."

"Agreed," said Zavonne.

"Well, maybe they're just scientists who have a lab in the warehouse and go sightseeing in their spare time."

"We used state-of-the-art DFEA imaging technology on these pictures," stated Zavonne briskly, "and these are the results."

Max stared as the screen showing the two figures in their motorbike helmets and balaclavas became pixelated. As the image refocused again, Max let out a gasp.

There staring back at him were two extremely fierce-looking *robots*.

MAX FLASH
MISSION 6

CHAPTER 3

Robot tourists! Mental – or should I say metal!

The tall robot had a sleek silver rectangular head with small oval eyes and a tiny circular nose. There was a series of light and dark green digital panels fixed across his throat. The small one had a larger circular head with square eyes. He had a series of opaque dials running down either side of his chin, like sideburns.

Their images disappeared and Zavonne's face reappeared in the mirror.

"These two are the most sophisticated robots the DFEA has ever come across," she informed Max. "They have made frequent visits to other locations in London, their appearance always preceded by a burst of magnetic waves. They then return to the warehouse where another set of magnetic waves signals their departure. Having digitally analyzed these waves, we believe these robots are using some sort of portal that takes them to and from a parallel world."

Robotsville? Excellent!

"But there is something else," said Zavonne.

"Yes?" said Max.

"When we managed to pick up fragments of their conversations we heard them refer to something they called 'Weapon Z'."

Max shivered.

"We're convinced they've developed a new deadly weapon and are staking out locations from which to launch their attack on our world."

"So you want me to investigate these robot guys?" asked Max.

Zavonne nodded.

"Your contortionist skills could come in very handy on a mission like this, and being smaller than an adult means you'll be far more able to disguise and hide yourself. That will probably be necessary, as we want you to travel through the portal into the robot world and find out exactly what it is they're planning."

Max met Zavonne's intense gaze.

Bring it on!

"We need you to find out where they come from, what kind of weapon they're developing and the significance of the locations they've visited. This information could be crucial to the survival of the human race."

So no pressure then!

"And you're going to give me robot-style gadgets, right?" asked Max, his eyes lighting up with anticipation.

"I will give you whatever gadgets I see fit," replied Zavonne sharply.

Sor-eee!

"There are three items inside the top drawer of your dressing table," said Zavonne.

Max pulled open the drawer and found three packages, labelled 1, 2 and 3.

"Open the first," commanded Zavonne.

Max placed packages 2 and 3 on the table and opened number 1. Inside were what looked like two green squishy juggling balls.

"Those are called SUCTION CREEPERS," explained Zavonne. "They will attach themselves to any surface, a wall for example, allowing the user to climb to the top. Their power lasts for sixty seconds."

Shinning up walls just like Spiderman – excellent!

"Now open the second one."

Inside was a wafer-thin mobile phone, flashier than any model Max had ever seen.

SUCTION CREEPERS

X2

0.20

0.20

40
30
20
10
KG
0   120   140   160

FLIP + TWIST MOBILE

0.60   0.60

0.100

CALL

20m   20m   0.200

BURN POINT PEN

0.60
0.20
300°c

0.200

0.100

0.100

"That is a FLIP + TWIST MOBILE," explained Zavonne. "When you flip the phone open and press the 'CALL' button, the microchip inside will undo any nuts, bolts and screws within a twenty metre radius."

Cool!

"The third gadget is a BURN POINT PEN."

Max pulled out what looked like an ordinary red pen.

"Click the button on top and the pen tip will produce enough heat to burn a hole in any material."

Fiendish!

"But remember, Max," cautioned Zavonne. "These gadgets may only be used in extreme situations or if your life is in danger."

"Yes, Zavonne," sighed Max. He'd heard this instruction a zillion times before!

"And there's just one more thing," Zavonne added. "In your wardrobe you'll find a warp-proof suit and helmet. The DFEA have developed this for all forms of interdimensional travel, which means you should be able to travel through the portal into the robots' world without any adverse effects."

Just then, Zavonne's phone rang and Max watched as she picked up the receiver. She listened in silence for a few seconds and then killed the call.

"We have just picked up a new set of magnetic waves," she said grimly. "This would seem to indicate that the robots have travelled through the portal and are with us once again. I want you to go to the warehouse immediately. A DFEA car will be here to pick you up in five minutes."

CHAPTER 4

Max ran to his parents' dressing room and explained the situation.

"I have to go," he said. "Zavonne's arranged for a car to pick me up outside the theatre."

"I guess you'll be missing school tomorrow then," sighed Mum, giving him a tight hug.

"Just take care," said Dad, squeezing Max on the shoulder. "You don't know what these robots are capable of."

"I'll be fine," Max reassured them. "Zavonne's given me some excellent gadgets and kit."

He found the warp-proof suit and helmet hanging in his wardrobe, as promised. They were made of shiny blue material and fitted tightly to his body. Once dressed, he then stuffed his gadgets in the suit's pockets.

Max hurried out of the theatre. It was late and a pale sliver of moon illuminated the dark sky. A black sedan with tinted windows was parked on the opposite kerb. He crossed the road and a door clicked open. He slid into the back seat. After a quick "hello" the DFEA driver said nothing, and thirty minutes later the car pulled up outside the gates of a large industrial park.

"It's the third unit along," said the driver.

Max thanked him and got out. The driver spun the car round and sped away.

Max strode down the wide road, past a printing workshop and a factory making industrial gloves. There was nobody else about.

The steel warehouse looked even bigger up close, and its large front entrance shutter was closed and padlocked. Slipping round the side, Max scanned the high walls for an entry point, but there was none. He hurried on to the back of the building and spotted a small air vent on top of a ledge, just above his head. He pulled himself up on to the ledge and quickly looked around. The whole place was dead.

He pulled off the wire mesh in front of the vent. Squashing his arms and legs into his body and tucking his head down towards his chest, he squeezed his way, feet first, through the vent and replaced the mesh behind him.

Max found himself on a ledge inside the building. He pulled out a torch and swung its beam across the walls. The warehouse was filled with floor-to-ceiling shelving units.

He jumped down and walked along the rows and rows of towering shelves. Every single one of them was empty.

No sign of their Weapon Z – unless of course it's invisible!

Suddenly the lights flickered to life and Max heard heavy footsteps. Quickly, he dived behind one of the units and peered out.

About fifty metres away he saw the two robots – one tall and sleek, and the other short and squat. Their faces gleamed with metallic menace.

MAX FLASH

"That's the last of the locations scouted, Krusher," said the shorter one. "We're now ready for the first deliveries."

"Excellent, Spike." The tall robot nodded. "Now let us return and attend to the final preparations."

The robots came to a halt about ten metres away from Max. He watched as Krusher pressed some kind of black key fob and a metallic circular panel on the warehouse floor raised by a metre.

The portal?

The robots stepped on to the panel.

Instantly, one of the warehouse's large ceiling lights swivelled in their direction and cast a brilliant white light on the circle. Its edges started to flash and a split second later the robots completely vanished.

The ceiling light was still focused on the circular panel, but Max could see the light starting to pulse and fade.

fffff

It's now or never!

He jumped out from his hiding place and leaped forward on to the panel.

A tingling sensation fizzed over his body and he felt himself being catapulted upwards at an unbelievable speed. Max closed his eyes and clenched his fists, as his stomach lurched.

Forget white-knuckle rides in theme parks – this is out of this world!

Suddenly Max came to a stop with a juddering halt.

He took a deep breath and opened his eyes.

MISSION 6

CHAPTER 5

Max was standing on a metallic circular
panel with a spotlight fixed above it,
identical to the one in the warehouse. He
jumped down off the panel and his eyes grew
to the size of plates as he gazed at the scene
in front of him.

The panel was set about fifteen metres back
from a huge thoroughfare. Sleek hovercars of
all different shapes, sizes and colours were
speeding silently by on both sides – all of them
driven by robots.

Max gulped.

*Looks like I'm the only human round here.
I stick out like a seriously sore thumb!*

At that moment he caught sight of Krusher
and Spike. They were standing by the kerb a
bit further down the road.

Max crept towards them.

Just then, a sleek silver hovercar pulled up.
Its doors slid open and the robots stepped
inside.

How am I going to follow them now?

Just as the car was pulling off, Max spotted
a yellow driverless vehicle with an AUTO TAXI
sign on its side.

Well, it's worth a try!

Max waved his hand in the air. To his
surprise, the taxi criss-crossed between the
other vehicles and skidded up to the kerb.

Its doors opened and Max quickly dived
in. Inside were two steel benches facing
each other.

"STATE DESTINATION!" demanded an automated voice.

"Er, follow that car!" said Max, hoping the vehicle would respond to his instruction. Luckily, it did. Its doors slid shut and it shot off. He slunk down in his seat, praying that he wasn't going to be spotted by a robot in another vehicle.

After a few minutes, Max's curiosity got the better of him and he stole a glance out of the window. Ahead was a huge four-tiered bridge

AUTO TAXI

carrying an assortment of gleaming vehicles. Along the side of the road giant billboards flashed past saying things like: REFRESHER OIL – LUBRICATES JOINTS THE OTHERS CAN'T REACH and RUST-PROOF INSURANCE CORP. A flying restaurant sped by, waiter robots zipping in and out of windows with orders.

In the distance loomed giant mirrored skyscrapers, a hundred times as tall as anything on earth. CYBER CITY – 5 MILES flashed a holographic sign on the roadside.

As the taxi entered the city, Max studied the many different kinds of robots walking down the pavements. It came to a halt at a set of traffic lights and Max watched as a robot threw a can out of a hovercar window. Instantly, metallic hands reached up from the tarmac and swept away the rubbish before retreating again as the lights changed and the cars pulled away.

Max tried to gather his thoughts.

OK, I need to get a robot disguise as quickly as possible. But where will I find one? There aren't going to be any shops selling them!

Max checked the progress of the car in front. It was pulling up against the kerb. A second later its two occupants got out. Max saw Krusher and Spike striding towards a gigantic skyscraper with a silver metal fist logo on its roof and the words SPR Command HQ emblazoned above the doors.

Promising! But what does SPR stand for?

Max's taxi cut past three vehicles, almost causing a huge pile-up, and pulled up at the kerb behind the silver hovercar.

"DESTINATION REACHED!" announced the automated voice.

"Er, thanks," said Max, getting to his feet.

The doors remained closed.

"Er, can I get out now, please?" asked Max, as he watched Krusher and Spike striding up the front steps of Command HQ.

"PAYMENT OF FARE NOT FORTHCOMING," declared the taxi.

Max groaned.

How am I going to pay the fare? I don't have any cash on me and even if I did it's hardly likely they'd accept human money here!

He watched anxiously as the two robots approached a massive security guard robot at the top of the steps.

"PAYMENT OF FARE NOT FORTHCOMING!" repeated the taxi.

Max looked on as the security guard dipped his head low and waved the two robots through.

They must be important.

A second later Krusher and Spike disappeared inside the building.

"PAYMENT OF FARE NOT FORTHCOMING!" said the taxi a third time.

There was only one thing for it. Max grabbed the edge of the door and using all his strength, started to prise it open.

"UNLAWFUL OPENING OF PASSENGER DOOR!" screamed the taxi, in a slightly hysterical, high-pitched voice. "REFRAIN FROM TOUCHING THE DOORS!"

But Max ignored the warning. Forcing the door open a fraction, he squashed his body through the gap and tumbled out on to the street. He ducked down behind a large silvery plant with sharp, spiked branches. Luckily, the security guard seemed not to have spotted him.

He was racking his brains for a way to get inside Command HQ without being seen when the taxi started bellowing a phrase over and over. "FARE EVADER ON THE LOOSE! FARE EVADER ON THE LOOSE! FARE EVADER ON THE LOOSE!"

MAX FLASH MISSION 6

A few seconds later Max heard the stomping of metal feet. He peered out and saw a huge robot with silver eyes, a blue light on its head and some kind of laser gun in a holster at its side pounding down the pavement in his direction.

A law enforcement official! Just what I DON'T want at the minute!

Without hesitating, Max dipped down an alley at the side of Command HQ. He could hear the stomping police robot behind him

as he ran to the end of the street. He took a
left, then a right, then another left. He reached
a junction and set off down a narrow alley on
his left.

He sprinted down the gloomy alley lined
with bins. It was a dead end.

Hearing the clunking footsteps of the police
robot fast approaching, Max ducked behind
one of the bins.

*Bit whiffy here, but it's better than being
caught, I guess!*

Max froze to the spot
as the robot marched
down the alley. Suddenly,
he felt something scuttle
over his foot. Gingerly,
he looked down and
saw what looked like
a grubby computer
mouse scuttle past.

I hope it doesn't byte!

Max listened as the robot's footsteps retreated into the distance. He waited a few more minutes until he was sure that the coast was clear and stood up. But just then a small white robot, about Max's size, with an orange light on its domed head, appeared round the corner. It was sweeping up rubbish with a large metal broom.

"Greetings," it said in a squeaky voice. "Please state your task."

Without thinking twice, Max leaped on to the robot and dragged it behind the bins.

A minute later, the police robot appeared at the entrance to the alley again. It stopped when it noticed a small robot sweeping up rubbish.

"Hey you!" it called. "Have you seen anyone running this way? I'm looking for a fare evader."

"No one identified," squeaked the robot.

"Something wrong with your voice box?" asked the police robot with a frown.

"No," replied the robot shakily, "just got a little cold."

"A cold what?" asked the police robot, but at that moment its walkie-talkie went. It looked suspiciously at the small robot, but then turned and marched back the way it had come.

Max breathed a heavy sigh of relief from inside the shell of the robot. His rapidly put-together disguise seemed to have worked. Luckily, the small robot hadn't put up much of a fight when Max had pounced on it. He'd had just enough time to activate its SHUT DOWN button, rip open a large panel on its back and dive inside its shell, hastily pulling the panel closed behind him.

The suit felt clunky and uncomfortable, but it was definitely better than being exposed as a human. There was a ventilation strip in the head which he could see through. Max knew he needed to blend in so he spent several minutes practising walking, and using his new robotic arms and hands. Max also worked on his new voice; trying hard to emulate the squeaky tones of his victim. When he was reasonably happy with this impersonation he set out to find Krusher and Spike.

But there was one small problem.

After all of the twists and turns he'd taken, he had no idea how to get back to Command HQ. And he didn't want to ask another robot for directions, at least not just yet. Trying to retrace his steps, he found himself on a wide, bustling street. Everywhere he looked, there were robots. Street vendors were selling steel burgers with microchips. Some robot children were throwing electrified glow-balls at each other that gave off an electric shock if they made contact with anything.

Max walked slowly, trying to figure out the way back to Command HQ, but there was no sign of it. He was considering his next move when he spotted a large, low-slung building that bore the metal fist logo – the same one he'd seen on the roof of Command HQ.

OK, this might not be my primary target, but there may well be something interesting inside that's connected to Command HQ and the robots' plans.

At once he began clunking towards the building.

MAX FLASH MISSION 6

CHAPTER 7

As Max approached the building, he saw a sign
stating ALL VISITORS REPORT TO RECEPTION.

*What reason can I give for being here?
Announcing I'm a human spy might not go
down too well!*

He took in his surroundings and saw a pile
of brown packages stacked on the side of a
loading bay. He hurried over and, making sure
no one was around, scooped up one of the
packages and headed to Reception.

Reception turned out to be a small room

with luminous yellow walls. Behind a glass desk Max could see a robot secretary inputting some data on to a minuscule laptop.

Max cleared his throat and rapped one of his robot fingers on the glass desk.

"Yes?" the secretary asked.

"I have a delivery," announced Max in his best robot voice, holding up the brown package.

"Department?"

"Excuse me?" said Max.

The robot rolled her eyes. "Which D-e-p-a-r-t-m-e-n-t is it for?" she asked in her most patronizing speaking-to-a-toddler voice.

Max thought quickly. He didn't know what went on inside this building, let alone what the departments were called.

"It's for the Department Department," Max said without thinking.

The secretary stared at him. "Never heard of it," she replied, folding her arms.

"That's because it's only just been set up," he responded. "As things are getting more departmentalized, the various departments decided they needed a new department called the Department Department for, you know, departmental things."

"Really?" the secretary said, with a suspicious glare.

"Well, it's been set up by Command HQ," said Max in desperation.

At the mention of Command HQ, however, her tone of voice changed.

"I've heard of it!" she said quickly. "I was just checking that you were a legitimate delivery robot."

"Of course I'm legitimate," said Max sharply, "now can I please go through and drop off this vital package? The Department Department requested I deliver it personally."

She nodded, then leaned forward and stuck a square magnet stating VISITOR on his chest. She flicked a switch and a door to Max's right swung open. He gave her a friendly wave and headed through.

The door led to a wide passage lit by bright white spotlights. Max passed several doors on each side, with signs reading "Iron Research and Development" and "Advanced Screwdriver Team". He turned right at the end of the passage and followed a flight of steps upwards. This took him to another corridor, at the end of

which was a set of double doors with a sign
stating: TOP SECRET. ENTRY RESTRICTED TO
AUTHORIZED PERSONNEL ONLY.

*Looks like as good a place as any to start
searching.*

Checking no one was around, Max pushed
open the doors and went through. He found
himself stepping on to a narrow walkway that
stretched high above a factory floor.

It was very hot, and Max immediately started
to sweat inside his robot suit. But at least the
place seemed empty.

At the end of the room was a roaring furnace. Every few seconds, molten metal streamed out, like lava from a volcano, into a series of moulds.

The moulds then snaked along a conveyer belt through a transparent tunnel. Inside, hundreds of metal hands assembled the pieces. From where he was standing, Max could just make out the finished silver objects as they emerged from the tunnel and dropped off the end of the conveyer belt into crates – each one stamped with a large letter "Z".

This must be where Weapon Z is being made! But what is it – some sort of gun?

Max headed across the walkway and leaned over the rail to try to get a closer look at the objects. He didn't spot the large metal hand extending from the ceiling to pick up the crates.

The hand only brushed against him, but this was enough to knock Max over the rail. He landed on the conveyer belt with a crashing of metal joints, and as he scrambled to get up one of his robotic legs got caught under the conveyer belt.

Frantically, he pulled at his robot leg, but it was totally stuck.

Just ahead was a large red lever. Max reached out with one hand and managed to slam it backwards. He gave a sigh of relief as the conveyer belt shuddered for a moment and seemed to come to a stop. But suddenly the belt started to move again – this time in reverse. He was heading straight for the furnace!

MISSION 6

CHAPTER 8

Max tried to wriggle out of his metal suit, but he couldn't reach the panel on the back. By now the furnace was only about fifteen metres away, and with each passing second he felt the baking heat increase.

Max grimaced.

I'm facing total meltdown!

The sweat poured off his face as the blasting furnace loomed ever nearer.

Ten metres to go. I'll be fried for sure.

Suddenly Max remembered the BURN

POINT PEN. Twisting from side to side he dislodged the pen from his pocket, and by bending backwards he tilted it towards his head. With a sharp nod, he jerked the pen out through the helmet's ventilation strip.

The heat was almost unbearable now. Max gripped the pen in his hand, stretched out and drew a line across the belt in front of him. Smoke trailed from the pen's nib.

The conveyer belt glowed red, then buckled, flinging Max through the air. He landed on the floor with a thud and lay there panting.

Phew! That was a lucky escape!

Max slowly got to his feet. He was just about to check out the weapons, when a shrill alarm sounded. "MACHINERY MALFUNCTION," screeched a robotic voice.

Not again!

Hearing the sound of running footsteps, Max stumbled over towards a door marked EXIT and pushed his way through. He found himself back on the main street.

OK, I didn't see what the weapons are, but I now know the robots are definitely making something. I need to get inside Command HQ and find out some more info!

This time the street was even more packed than before, and Max found himself caught up in a crowd of robots. Some were carrying banners and others shaking rattles.

As Max was swept along by the crowd, he heard the sound of chanting and clapping. There in front of him towered a giant stadium, with the words CYBER CITY in glowing green letters.

Shame I haven't got time to check out a major robot sporting event!

But a second later, Max spotted Krusher and Spike. They were being driven in their sleek silver hovercar towards the gates of the stadium. The crowds parted to let them through. The car swept past a line of stewards and straight into the stadium.

If they were here to watch a game, Max was going to watch it too!

He joined the crowd and walked under a large arch into the stadium. Ahead of him was a great throng of robots. Some were drinking frothing grey liquid from large tankards; others were heading straight to their seats.

But there was one problem. To reach the inside of the stadium you had to pass through

one of fifty automated ticket barriers and Max
had no ticket. No ticket meant no game; no
game meant losing Krusher and Spike again.

I MUST get in!

Max watched the crowds for a few moments
and eventually spotted a family of five trying to
make their way through one of the barriers.
Their smallest child, a small mauve and white
robot with goofy, jagged teeth, had sneaked
back through the barrier, which then closed
again denying him access. One of the stewards
beckoned the family to come to a barrier at the
far end. The steward had a key for this and
held the gate open.

Max saw his chance. He hurried towards the
gate, nipped ahead of the robot child and
passed through.

"Oy! Stop!" shouted the steward, but Max
was already lost in the crowd of supporters.

Woo-hoo! I've made it!

Max looked around and saw Krusher and

Spike climbing some steps that led to Block 4. He hurried after them and found himself inside the arena.

There were banks upon banks of seats looking out over the bright-green rubber pitch. A massive screen stood at each corner of the stadium to provide replays and clips of legendary games.

Max hurried down the stairs and spotted a free seat just behind Krusher and Spike, six rows from the front.

I never get seats this good when I go to football matches back home!

Max sat down and tried to listen in to their conversation over the chatter of the crowd.

"Are you sure we should be here, Krusher?" said Spike, the smaller robot.

"I'm not missing this match for anything!" snapped Krusher. "Anyway, this is as good a place as any to pick up some recruits to help us with the final stages of our Great Plan."

Great Plan?

Max leaned forwards to try to hear more. But just as he did so, a gigantic purple robot in the seat behind stood up and loomed over him.

"What do you think YOU'RE doing here?" it demanded, pointing an accusing metal finger.

MAX FLASH
MISSION 6

CHAPTER 9

Max gulped nervously and looked around
wildly for an escape route.

*Has my back panel come off? Does he know
I'm a human in disguise?*

The robot grabbed him by the shoulder and
pulled him to his feet.

"Tier 96 is your section," it told him crossly,
"that's where you need to be."

Max was about to ask why he belonged in
Tier 96, but he didn't want to draw any more
attention to himself, so he edged past the

other supporters. Spotting Tier 96 right at the top of Block 4, he hurried up the steps. The first thing he noticed was that all the robots sitting there were identical to him; they had the same white shell and orange light on the top of their dome-shaped head.

Maybe we're the away supporters?

Max squeezed past three robots and placed himself on an empty seat.

"It's great going to other teams' stadiums, isn't it?" he said to the robot on his left, testing out this theory. "You know – being an away supporter?"

The robot swivelled round and fixed him with a weird look. "This is the home section," it said sharply. "If you want the away section it's in Block 25."

"Of course!" Max nodded quickly. "I was only joking. I'm the world's biggest Cyber City fan!"

The crowd suddenly roared as the two teams came out on to the pitch. Each one had ten players – all massive, all shaking their fists at each other.

"Who are we playing again?" said Max to the robot beside him.

"Bolt United," replied the robot sharply.

Max looked at the pitch and noticed there wasn't a ball anywhere in sight. A buzzer sounded and Max immediately saw the reason for the lack of a ball. It seemed that the object of the game was for the robot players to attack each other. The crashing of metal against metal rang through the stadium, and the roar of the crowd accompanied each and every collision. The details of the match were continually updated on the jumbo screens.

Direct Belly Hits: United 7 – City 3

Head-On Collisions: United 4 – City 4

Butt Kicks: United 6 – City 2

Max kept looking out for Krusher and Spike, but found himself being swept up in the action. Soon he was cheering and shouting like all of the other robots in Tier 96.

He therefore didn't spot Krusher and Spike rapidly climbing up the steps towards Tier 96, and pointing towards him and his neighbours.

A split second later, Max felt a jolt as the bottom of his seat dropped away and he found himself falling into blackness.

MAX FLASH
MISSION 6

CHAPTER 10

As Max's eyes got used to the gloom, he saw
he was plummeting towards a large open-top
truck. He landed in a crumpled heap, and
moments later his fellow supporters from the
stadium tumbled down on top of him.

As he untangled himself from the others,
Max noticed that in front of him stood a neat
row of identical robots.

"OK, let's get moving!" he heard a voice shout
from outside, and the truck's roof slid shut.

Max cursed himself.

Why wasn't I more careful? I need to get to Command HQ and now I'm trapped! Did Krusher and Spike see through my disguise? But if so what are these other robots from the stadium doing here?

Some of the robots were whispering to each other about the match and the superiority of Cyber City. Max looked gloomily at the robot facing him.

"What's going on?" he asked.

The robot frowned at him. "Same as usual," it replied.

"The usual being?"

"We were allowed out for the day to watch the match, but we've been recalled before the end."

"What have we been let out of?" asked Max.

"Are you in denial?" asked the robot with suspicion. "We're drones, *remember*? We serve wherever we're directed. That's what comes with being in the lowest level of society."

Drones? The lowest level of society?

Max could have hit himself. That was why he'd been directed to Tier 96 in the stadium. It was reserved for drones – the lowest of the low!

Why couldn't I have stolen the shell of a robot VIP?

"But look on the bright side," said another drone. "This isn't any old job we've been recalled for. This is the Big One!"

"What's that?" asked Max.

"We're about to find out!" replied the drone enthusiastically.

Max groaned. *That's helpful! What a nightmare! Now I'll never get near Command HQ and the robots will unleash their terrifying weapon on humans ... whatever it is!*

Suddenly the drone opposite Max shouted, "Is everyone up for this?"

The answers came quickly.

"Totally!"

"Wicked!"

"Right on!"

They were all brimming with excitement. Max shook his head in disbelief.

These guys are actually looking forward to being servants!

After another few minutes the vehicle pulled to a halt. The back doors of the truck opened, and Max and the other drones streamed out into a large, airy room and formed a neat line.

"Drones!" called out a powerful and throaty voice from somewhere.

The drones bowed their heads low.

A second later, Krusher and Spike stepped into the room. They were followed by vicious-looking robodog, which started snapping at the heels of the drones. A trail of oily goo dripped from its steel jaws.

"Heel, Metal Meathead!" commanded Spike. The dog obediently stopped attacking the drones' feet and ran over to his master's side.

Metal Meathead? That doesn't sound like a gentle pet!

"Welcome, drones!" declared Krusher. "Welcome to Command HQ!"

Command HQ?

Max couldn't believe his metal ears. Finally he'd made it. Yes, he was here as a servant, but at least he'd get a chance to look for clues about what was actually going on.

Being a drone has got me just where I want to be!

"Right," declared Krusher. "I have important business to deal with so Spike will show you to your task. The time for the Great Plan is nearly upon us!" With that, Krusher turned and disappeared somewhere inside the building.

What IS the Great Plan? If I don't find out soon, my mission will be a total wipeout!

"Now listen up, drones!" said Spike sharply. "You are to carry out this task with the utmost drone diligence."

"Yes, Master Spike," chirped the drones. "We will carry it out with the utmost drone diligence!"

"And bear this in mind," hissed Spike menacingly. "Metal Meathead here doesn't take kindly to shirkers, gossipers or robots with a bad attitude. Understand?"

"Yes, Master Spike," responded the drones.

"You are to prepare the delivery lorries. They must be emptied out and made spick and span!"

"Most definitely, Master Spike!" trilled the drones.

He clapped his hands and the drones followed Spike, with Max hurrying to keep up. Metal Meathead brought up the rear.

They marched through a large door and down some steps into a wide courtyard at the back of the building.

Ahead sat a line of lorries. Spike quickly split the drones up into pairs.

"Right," he said, "begin your clear-out. I'm leaving Metal Meathead here to keep an eye on you."

And with that Spike headed back into the building.

"I'm Max," whispered Max to the drone he had been paired with. "What's your name?"

"I'm Snap," the drone replied, looking slightly confused. "Now let's get started," he added earnestly.

They walked round to the back of their first lorry. Methodically they began to clear out the junk from inside – mostly rusty old tools and damaged computer terminals.

"What's going to go in these lorries?" Max asked Snap.

"Our job is to do, not to question," answered Snap.

"But you must know something?"

"Our brains only store data relevant to our immediate tasks," replied Snap.

Max sighed. If he couldn't prise anything out of Snap, he'd just have to start searching for himself. He glanced over towards the building. Metal Meathead was standing directly in front of the door, slavering and keeping his beady eyes fixed on the drones.

I don't fancy a run-in with Meathead! I need to find something that will keep a robodog occupied.

Max hunted through the lorry and pulled out a rusty spanner.

Suppose this will have to do...

"Hey, Snap," he called, "I'm going to take a short break."

Snap gazed at him blankly. "What's a break?"

"It's a ... don't worry about it," Max said. "My joints just need a bit of a stretch."

"An unauthorized move, how irregular," said Snap, puzzled. "Well, don't be long."

"I won't," replied Max, walking towards the building. When he was about twenty metres away from Metal Meathead, he launched the spanner through the air to the far side of the courtyard.

"Fetch!"

The robodog watched it spin through the air and immediately gave chase.

MAX FLASH

Max ran towards the door, hoping the bait had bought him enough time. But just as he was reaching out for the handle, he heard a bloodcurdling growl from behind.

MAX FLASH
MISSION 6

Max watched in horror as Metal Meathead leaped through the air at him. He yanked the door open as hard as he could, smashing it into the dog and propelling him backwards.

Max dived through the door and pulled it firmly shut behind him. He heard Metal Meathead run at the door and start pawing at it, yelping in frustration.

That was close!

His heart still racing, Max crept down the corridor. To his right was a glass lift.

Max stepped inside and scanned the gleaming silver buttons, which ran from "Basement: Drone Zone" through to "Floor 101: Control Centre".

Interesting...

He touched the button for 101 and the doors slid shut. Max was shot upwards at phenomenal speed. Seconds later the lift jolted to a halt. He stepped out ... and walked straight into Spike.

"What are YOU doing here?"

Spike was carrying a large, wafer-thin TV screen.

"Just liaising with the packing team," blurted out Max, trying to keep to his best drone voice. "I must have got the wrong floor."

"Liaising!" cried Spike. "You're a drone! Your job is not to liaise! Who sent you here?"

"Krusher!" blurted out Max.

Spike sighed. "OK, make yourself useful and take this screen to the Viewing Room on your

way down. You need to fix it up on the wall –
think you can manage that? The room's on
floor 26. Make sure you get the right place
this time."

He handed Max the TV screen, which was
heavier than it looked. Max staggered
backwards.

"Well, get a move on!" shouted Spike,
pushing Max back into the lift.

*I need to check out that Control Centre, but
there's no chance with Spike around. I'll drop
off the screen and hopefully he'll be gone by
the time I return.*

As the lift descended, Max heard a loud
announcement on a tannoy system.

"ALL DRONES REPORT TO THE VIEWING
ROOM IMMEDIATELY! ALL DRONES REPORT
TO THE VIEWING ROOM IMMEDIATELY!"

Max got out of the lift on floor 26 and a few
moments later saw a whole line of drones
marching towards a blue door. He followed

them inside and spotted a cable protruding from the wall. Hoisting the screen on to his shoulder, Max climbed up on to a small stepladder and connected the screen.

More and more drones were arriving and within minutes the room was full. They stood in neat lines awaiting the start of the broadcast. Max joined the back row and found himself next to Snap.

The letters SPR filled the screen.

"What's that?" Max whispered.

"The Society for the Protection of Robots, of course," answered Snap. "You must know that!"

"Greetings, drones," said a presenter's voice, "and welcome to your final instruction broadcast. We know you have far below average robot intelligence, but even you should get the gist of what's about to follow."

Max looked around at the drones, whose faces were glued to the screen.

"In thirty minutes the final stage of our Great Plan will be put into action and we will travel to 'The Other Side' as conquerors!"

There was a cheer from the collected drones. Max gulped. *Conquerors!*

"We must never forget the reason for this quest," said the voice.

The screen was filled with pictures of humans constructing robots on assembly lines and then putting them inside cars that were

smashed against walls. The next images
showed children with toy robots. The children
flung them around and even pulled off the
robots' limbs.

The drones booed at the images on the
screen.

"That is how they treat us!" snarled the
presenter's voice. "So revenge will be sweet!"

The drones cheered and gave each other
high fives.

OK, thought Max. *They believe that humans
mistreat them, so they want to get their own
back using their Weapon Z to conquer Earth.
But I need to find out exactly what this is –
and fast!*

Max turned and started tiptoeing towards
the door. All of the drones were still staring up
at the screen.

All except one.

"Hey, where are you going? We've been
instructed to watch the entire programme."

Max spun round.

It was Snap.

"I've been assigned to another task," said Max, still edging towards the door.

"Really?" asked Snap. "What kind of task?"

"I'd love to tell you," whispered Max furtively, "but it's top secret."

"But drones' work is never top secret," pointed out Snap, raising his voice. "One unauthorized move is bad, BUT TWO IS UNACCEPTABLE!"

Hearing Snap's outburst, the other drones turned round to see what was going on. Max was right by the door now, but Snap stepped forward and blocked his way. A split second later, the drones all started moving in on him.

MISSION 6

CHAPTER 13

As the drones surrounded Max they started chanting.

"Our aim is to serve!"

"Obey and follow!"

"Respond to orders!"

"No unauthorized moves!"

"They think, drones do!"

"I'm not your average drone," replied Max coolly, before shoulder-barging the nearest drone, who toppled into the others.

Max sprinted across the room and climbed

up on to the stepladder. The drones got to
their feet and chased after him. Soon he was
surrounded again, but this was exactly what
Max wanted. Grabbing the TV screen from the
wall, he launched himself off the stepladder
and used the drones' domed heads as stepping
stones back towards the exit.

He dived off the last drone's head and sailed
through the doorway. He slammed the door and
used the screen to jam it shut behind him, then
raced off down the corridor.

He reached the lift and slammed the button for floor 101.

Time to check out that Control Centre!

Max stepped out of the lift and as he reached the large metal door to the Control Centre, he could hear voices from inside. It was Krusher and Spike.

Max crouched down and peered through the keyhole.

"So you have the complete list of destinations?" Krusher was asking.

"Affirmative," replied Spike.

"Once we have all of our foot soldiers in place, I will be able to control their every move with this Activation Pod!" Krusher pulled out a shiny black object shaped like an egg. On the top was a gleaming silver button.

"I can't wait for tonight's big show in the square." Krusher laughed.

The square? Does he mean another portal, but square, not round this time?

Suddenly Max saw Metal Meathead running towards the door.

Yikes!

He ducked down.

Metal Meathead started pawing at the door.

"What is it, Meathead?" demanded Spike suspiciously, walking over to the door.

Max turned and fled. Luckily, the room next door was unlocked and he dived inside. It appeared to be some kind of research lab. He listened as the door to the Control Centre clicked open.

The moment Meathead was released he caught Max's scent and bounded over to the lab door, barking furiously.

"There's something in there," said Spike, reaching out for the door handle.

"LEAVE IT!" ordered Krusher. "We need to get going. Time is of the essence."

Max heard the sound of the Control Centre door being locked and then the howling of Metal Meathead as he was dragged off down the corridor.

While he waited to make sure the coast was clear, he reached his arm down inside his robot suit and fumbled through his pockets to find something to use to unlock the door.

Chewing gum wrapper ... no. Piece of string ... not really. Used tissue ... I don't think so!

Just then, he spotted an air vent on the wall. He climbed up on to one of the lab benches to investigate.

Through the vent Max had a perfect view of the Control Centre.

The walls of the room were lined with giant computer screens. There was a map of London covered in hundreds of large red dots. On the

next screen he could just make out a list
of words: Andertons, Kethwicks, Cooper
and Gates."

Andertons?

The name rang a bell for Max, but he
couldn't quite think where he'd heard it
before.

In the centre of the room was a glass table
and on this Max spotted a shiny black egg-
shaped object with a gleaming silver button
on top.

*The Activation Pod! I've got to get my
hands on that!*

Max pulled off the grate of the air vent and
scrambled up the wall. In the robot suit it was
a tight squeeze to get through, but he just
made it, falling to the floor with a loud
CLANG!

He was just about to reach for the Activation
Pod when the door was flung open and Spike
marched in. He stared in surprise at the drone.

"How did you get in here?" demanded Spike, snatching up the Activation Pod.

"I was directed here by Krusher," replied Max.

"Krusher would *never* authorize a drone to be in this section of the building," snapped Spike.

Max realized this trick wasn't going to work on Spike a second time, so he opted for another strategy.

"Salad, dustbin, fish and chips," he blurted out.

"What did you say?" asked an incredulous looking Spike.

"Shopping, nostrils, soup," added Max. He then bashed into a chair, reversed and crashed into it again.

Spike shook his head and pulled out a mobile phone.

Max spun round a couple of times and started chanting nursery rhymes.

"Incy wincy spider..."

"I have a malfunctioning drone over at Command HQ," Spike snarled into the phone. "I need D-Squad here immediately."

He listened for a few seconds.

"Yes, yes," he said impatiently, casting a quick glance at Max. "Just make sure you bring the right vehicle for drone disposal!"

MAX FLASH
MISSION 6
CHAPTER 14

Max gulped. *That doesn't sound good!*

"Hurry up!" ordered Spike, pushing Max out of the Control Centre into a service lift. The lift shot down and Max found himself back out in the courtyard.

The lorries from before were now fully prepared and Max watched as drones climbed into the cabs and powered up the engines. The main gates swung open, and one by one the lorries pulled away.

Then he heard the roar of a very large engine

as a huge orange truck snaked round the corner and pulled into the courtyard. Three massive oval-headed robots climbed out. They had the words D-SQUAD sprayed across their chests in orange letters.

"At last," said Spike, shoving Max in the direction of the robots. "Deal with this malfunctioning drone at once!"

With that Spike hurried back inside the building. The largest of the D-Squad robots bent down and stuck his face in Max's. "So what have we got here then? A drone that doesn't do exactly what its master tells it to?"

"Actually, I'm not malfunctioning at all," said Max, quickly. "There's ... there's been a mix up with another drone. It's inside the building. I can show it to you."

Max spun round and began marching back towards the building, but a metal arm grabbed him by the neck and pulled him back.

"We're not buying that one, are we, lads?" the huge robot chuckled.

"No way!" chorused the other two.

"You see, you're going to treat us to a spectacular show," explained the first robot. "The crunching of metal, the grinding of joints. We wouldn't miss it for the world. We like to see drones going in whole and coming out like crushed cans!"

"Call it recycling!" sniggered one of the other robots.

"But you've got it wrong!" shouted Max. "I function perfectly. Go on, give me an instruction."

But D-Squad weren't having any of it. The largest robot picked up Max, slung him over his shoulder and marched to the back of the truck. Max's eyes nearly popped out of their sockets when he saw the gleaming metal teeth.

"Rev her up!" shouted the robot. The other two hopped into the cab. The engine roared and the terrifying teeth came to life, chomping up and down with swift crunching motions.

"In you go!" laughed the big robot. "We'll see you on the other side!"

He lifted Max high into the air and prepared to feed him to the huge, gnashing teeth.

MISSION 6

CHAPTER 15

If ever there was a time for the FLIP + TWIST MOBILE, it was now. A split second before Max was fed to the hungry D-Squad truck's teeth, he whipped out the phone from his pocket, flipped it open and pressed the CALL button. In an instant every single nut and bolt within a twenty-metre radius came undone. It was chaos!

The three D-Squad robots fell apart. The D-Squad truck collapsed in a metallic heap. The main gates toppled over.

And Max's robot shell fell to bits around him.

Ooops! That wasn't supposed to happen.

He'd saved himself from the jaws of the vicious truck, but now Max was fully exposed as a human. He wouldn't last for long around here if he was spotted.

Max jumped over the collapsed gates, sprinted down the side of the building and emerged on to the main street. He caught sight of Krusher, Spike and Metal Meathead climbing into their silver car. There was no way he was going to go for the fare evader option again, so there was only one thing for it. He raced towards the car. In one massive leap he threw himself on to the roof, just as it started to pull away.

"HEY!" shouted a robot couple in the street, staring at the human in astonishment.

But they were too late to do anything; the car was already racing through the traffic. Max lay flat on the roof and held on tight.

The car sped down the street, cutting up other vehicles. As it approached its destination, Max instantly recognized the large circular metal panel of the portal. But this time the light's beam was much broader and stronger than before. Max watched as a queue of silver Command HQ lorries drove into the glow and disappeared one by one.

The car pulled up and Krusher, Spike and Metal Meathead got out. They headed straight for the portal. Max slid off the roof and looked on as they stepped into the light.

As the beam began to fade, there was just enough time for him to run up and dive through.

He felt the same tingling sensation as before

and his stomach flipped over. Moments later
he found himself back in the warehouse in his
own world ... lying at the feet of Krusher.

Krusher lunged forward and dragged Max up
by the scruff of his neck.

"So what have we here ... a human spy?"

CHAPTER 16

"How did you enter our world, you repulsive human?" demanded Krusher with a terrifying snarl.

"I work for a human—robot travel agency," replied Max, gulping as Spike and Metal Meathead moved menacingly towards him. "We need to update our brochures so I thought I'd just pay you guys a visit and—"

"SILENCE!" barked Krusher.

Max looked around the warehouse. Whereas before the shelves had been empty, they were now crammed full of steel crates, each stamped with the letter "Z".

All the time I've been in the robot world they must have been shipping their weapons here!

A team of drones was loading the crates from the shelves into the back of the large silver lorries.

"TIME FOR YOU LOT TO HIT THE ROAD!" Krusher ordered, as he dragged Max across the room.

Instantly the drones started pulling down the steel shutters on the backs of the lorries and clambering inside. They twisted the ignition keys and gunned their engines. There was a loud buzz as the warehouse gates opened. A moment later the lorries started pouring out.

"OVER HERE, SPIKE!" shouted Krusher. "And bring me a crate."

As Spike struggled over with one of the crates, Krusher turned his attentions back to Max.

"So you wish to ruin our Great Plan, do you?"

"OK," said Max, "the tourist thing was a lie. I'm ... I'm ... really a health and safety officer. I'm ... I'm doing a check on all metallic dogs. You need a special licence to have one."

"Do you think I was born yesterday?" Krusher snarled furiously.

"I don't know," replied Max, "were you?"

"You INSOLENT human!" Krusher shouted. "You are a SPY and spies must be dealt with." He turned to Spike. "Open that crate!" he ordered.

Max took a deep breath.

This is it! The moment I've been waiting for! I'm finally going to get to see the terrifying weapon they've created! I just hope they're not about to try it out on me.

Max watched intently as Spike slid the top panel of the crate open.

Is it a bomb? Is it a laser gun?

Spike reached into the box and lifted something out.

But it wasn't a gun or a bomb or anything remotely like a weapon.

It was a model robot. It had large silver eyes and a shiny blue chrome body covered in high-tech circuitry. It stood around ten centimetres tall.

Max couldn't believe his eyes. He burst out laughing. "That's it? That's your incredible new weapon to attack the human race – a crummy little toy?"

MISSION 6

CHAPTER 17

Krusher shot Max a furious look. "You want to see how crummy it is?" he screamed. "Let me show you!" He tore off the packaging.

Max stopped laughing.

Maybe it wasn't so funny after all.

"Er, how does it work?" asked Max, staring at the toy. "Is it some kind of bomb?"

"Oh, human fool!" hissed Krusher, leaning in towards Max. "Do you really think we'd be able to achieve our aims using a conventional weapon?"

"So what does it do?" asked Max.

"These little beauties are called Z-Bots," Krusher informed Max, "and their favourite pastime is playing with human brains – particularly CHILDREN'S brains! You see, when the children of your world get their greedy hands on these I will switch on the Activation Pod. Then each and every child will fall under my control."

"You're not serious, are you?" said Max.

"You'd better believe it," snarled Krusher. "They will be my army of mindless and willing slaves – ready to take over the world! And seeing as you're so interested in how the Z-Bots work, I think it's time for a trial run— OOOOWWW!"

At that moment, Max stamped hard on Krusher's foot.

Krusher released Max from his grip, and he sprinted towards a narrow gap between two of the shelving units and squeezed himself into it.

"FIND THAT HUMAN CHILD!" Krusher screamed.

Max peered out from behind the shelves. A couple of drones were loading crates into the last of the lorries.

I have to follow that lorry!

Max edged out a fraction, but just as he was about to make a run for it, he felt a tug at his leg. He looked down.

It was Metal Meathead.

Max put a finger to his lips. "Good boy," he whispered, "I'm your friend."

Unfortunately, Meathead's affections couldn't be won that easily and he started gnawing at Max's trousers.

"Get off!" hissed Max, desperately trying to escape. But the savage robodog wasn't the only thing he had to worry about. A split second later he heard footsteps rapidly approaching.

"GOTCHA!" shouted a triumphant Spike.

"OVER HERE, KRUSHER!"

Spike grabbed Max's arm while Meathead took care of his leg and together they dragged him out from behind the unit. Max tried to wriggle free, but he was no match for their combined metallic strength.

Krusher marched over with the Z-Bot. He tossed it to Spike, who held it up in front of Max's face. Krusher then whipped out the Activation Pod and pressed the silver button. The pod split in half and an aerial extended. Krusher pressed another button and the toy robot's eyes began to glow amber.

Max gazed into the robot's eyes, transfixed.

"Relax," came the voice of Krusher. It sounded muffled and echoey.

Max felt a dull sensation in his head and his limbs grew heavy. He slumped forwards.

I'm being hypnotized!

Max had spent years watching magicians who specialized in mind manipulations. He was aware that in a matter of seconds he'd be totally under the Z-Bot's spell.

He focused his brain and started repeating the mantra, "Stop the brain flow, stop the brain flow—"

"JUMP!" commanded Krusher.

Although he tried to resist, Max found himself springing up and down.

"Stop the brain flow, stop the brain flow, stop the brain flow."

As he continued to jump, he kept on repeating this, fighting to regain control of his mind. Gradually his thoughts came back into focus. He was himself again.

However, as far as Krusher and Spike were concerned, he was totally under their spell. And he was going to play along with their instructions.

"DANCE!" said Krusher.

Max leaped through the air, then pirouetted as if he was a fully-paid-up member of the world's finest ballet troupe.

"BE A DOG!" ordered Spike.

Max got on to all fours and started panting. He barked at Metal Meathead, who growled back ferociously.

"EXCELLENT!" laughed Krusher, pressing a sequence of buttons on the Activation Pod. "Our victims will do exactly what we tell them to do!" He turned back to Max. "Now sleep."

Max stood rooted to the spot, a glazed, vacant look on his face.

"Right, Meathead," said Krusher. "We have deliveries to supervise. We'll return for you shortly."

Meathead dribbled.

"As for the human," said Krusher dismissively, "you have one simple task."

Meathead looked up eagerly.

"Finish him off!" hissed Krusher.

MAX FLASH MISSION 6

CHAPTER 18

Krusher and Spike hurried across the warehouse, jumped on to a motorbike and sped off. Max was surprised to see they hadn't bothered with their disguises.

As soon as they'd gone, he snapped out of his pretend trance and eyed the dog.

"I guess it's just you and me now, Meathead old boy," said Max nervously, as the robodog tugged at his trouser leg.

"Look," said Max, "I know we got off to a bad start, but I'm sure we can work this out."

Metal Meathead shook his head.

"Come on, Meathead!" said Max to the evil robodog. "I can get you a far tastier meal than me! I'll find you some nice juicy bolts – how about it?"

Meathead started barking furiously.

In a lightning quick manoeuvre, Max kicked out and sent Meathead flying across the warehouse floor.

Meathead picked himself up and prepared to lunge at Max again.

I can't keep this up for ever!

So Max took the only other option – he ran.

With Metal Meathead in close pursuit, he sprinted towards the nearest shelving unit, swerved round a corner and found himself in another aisle. He upped his pace and put a tiny bit more distance between himself and the metal mutt, his mind working furiously on methods of escaping Meathead's snapping jaws. But he groaned as he reached the end of the aisle.

It was a dead end.

There was nowhere else to run and he didn't fancy his chances in another one-on-one battle with the savage metal canine.

It was then he spotted a gap between the shelving unit and the wall. He squeezed sideways into the space as Metal Meathead tore down the aisle towards him.

Max tugged at the shelving unit.

It didn't budge, so he tried again more forcefully. This time it moved. The unit wobbled for a second and fell towards the floor. Metal Meathead froze as he saw the unit looming over him, then yelped and frantically tried to backtrack.

But he was too late.

The unit smashed down on top of the robodog and Max heard a loud crunch as he was squashed flat.

Max had no time to dwell on Metal Meathead's demise. He had a far more vital mission. He ran back into the main section of the warehouse where the last lorry was parked. Its rear door was still open.

Max ran towards the lorry and dived into the back, a split second before a drone appeared to slam down the shutter.

Phew! I don't think he saw me. But he will when he empties out the crates!

Then Max had an idea. He turned to the nearest crate and prised off the lid.

The crate was packed with Z-Bots. Max pulled them out and stuffed them behind the pile of crates at the back of the lorry. When only a few Z-Bots remained, he then climbed into the crate and piled the Z-Bots on top of him so that he'd be hidden when the crate was opened. He pulled the lid firmly shut.

It was a bumpy ride but Max was too busy thinking to notice.

OK, so they have thousands of these Z-Bots that they're going to use to hypnotize children and turn them into an army. But how are they going to get them into the children's hands? And aren't people going to be suspicious if they see a load of robots running around London?

A short while later the lorry stopped and Max heard the voice of Krusher.

"This is the last delivery," he said. "I hope everything is in order."

The lorry's rear shutter opened and Max felt his crate being lifted up in the air.

"Weird!" he heard Spike say. "This one feels much heavier than the others!"

Max held his breath, worried that Spike might open the crate.

"Just get on with it!" Krusher shouted.

Max slid around inside the crate as it was

carried up some steps. In the distance he could hear excited cheering and clapping. Finally, his crate was plonked down.

"Could you just sign for these?" he heard Krusher ask.

"Of course!" giggled a female voice. "You do look fetching in that outfit!"

"Thank you, Madam!" replied Krusher. "It's all part of the service!"

Max prayed his crate wasn't the first to be opened. He was lucky. He heard crates being prised open to gasps of surprise and delight. A couple of minutes later, he heard his crate lid being levered and a beam of light hit his eyes as the Z-Bots above him were taken out of the box.

He came face to face with a young woman.

"AAAAARRRRRGGGGHHHH!" she screamed.

MAX FLASH
MISSION 6

CHAPTER 19

"Don't worry!" said Max, scrambling to his feet. He quickly checked to see if Krusher and Spike were still around – they'd gone. He stepped out of the crate on to a counter, then jumped to the floor.

He was in a shop – ANDERTONS TOYS read a sign.

That's where I'd heard the name Andertons before! This is the biggest toyshop in London.

Outside the shop was a very long and highly excitable queue of children.

"I like your outfit," said the shop assistant, taking in Max's warp-proof suit. "Are you part of the promotion, too?"

"Promotion?" asked Max.

She pointed behind him. He turned round and was greeted by the sight of a huge film poster hanging on the wall. It showed Krusher and Spike. The title of the film was: REVENGE OF THE KILLER ROBOTS.

Max's mouth dropped open.

"This film promotion," she said. "The world premiere is tonight!"

So that's how the robots are managing to avoid suspicion. They're making it seem like they're "dressed up" as robots as part of the marketing drive for a film.

"And these Z-Bots?" added Max. "They're also part of the marketing?"

"Of course!" The woman laughed. "The company who made the film are giving a free Z-Bot to every kid in the city. That's why all the toy stores are staying open tonight! Isn't it exciting!"

So that's why Krusher and Spike had visited those locations all over London; they must have been checking out all of the toyshops and planning their Z-Bot drop-off routes!

"When does the premiere start?" demanded Max urgently.

"At seven o'clock," she answered.

Max looked down at his watch. It was 6.45 p.m.

"Where is it?"

"Leicester Square," she replied.

"You don't have a spare ticket, do you?"

Max gulped. Krusher had said something about "the square". But he didn't mean a square shape, he meant Leicester Square! In twenty-five minutes every kid in London would have their own Z-Bot. All Krusher needed to do then was to activate the machines with his Pod, hypnotize his huge army of children and get them to carry out his orders against the unsuspecting adults. It wouldn't be long before the whole city was under his evil control.

"I've got to go," he said. "Whatever you do, do NOT give those Z-Bots out."

"Hang on a moment, who are you—" the shop assistant began. But at that second, one of the other store assistants opened the main doors and a huge crowd of children ran into the shop, fighting and pushing to get their hands on their free Z-Bots.

Max groaned as he imagined an identical scene taking place at every toyshop in London.

MISSION 6

CHAPTER 20

Max pushed through the crowd of kids.

I'm never going to make it!

He had fifteen ... no, fourteen minutes before Krusher activated the Z-Bots.

Just as he reached the shop doors Max noticed a display of mini micro scooters.

"Mind if I borrow this?" he shouted behind him as he grabbed a bright blue scooter.

Woo hoo!

Pedestrians dived out of the way as Max shot through the automatic shop doors and across

the pavement. He
knew the way to
Leicester Square
because it was right
near the Royal
Theatre where he'd
performed his
magic show.

*But it's much
more fun getting
there this way than
by walking!*

Max reached
Leicester Square at
precisely 6.51 p.m.

I have nine minutes to avert disaster!

Abandoning the scooter, he weaved through
the throng of children and parents gathered
around the legendary Coronet Cinema, which
was hung with huge banners advertising
REVENGE OF THE KILLER ROBOTS.

As he jostled his way through to the front, he saw with panic that every single child was clutching a Z-Bot!

"Hey, watch out!" someone snapped, but he ignored them and ploughed on. Once at the front, he craned his neck and saw the red carpet. A horde of photographers were popping flashbulbs.

But there was no sign of Krusher or Spike.

Maybe they're inside already.

Max checked out the guests flashing official invites at the line of security guards.

There's no chance I'll get in that way!

He turned and scanned the rest of the square. That was when he saw them.

High up on the roof of a towering building on the other side of the square were Krusher and Spike. Max could see the Activation Pod in Krusher's hands. Time was running out.

Fighting his way back through the crowd, Max hared across the square to the tall building. As he approached it, he saw that the front doors were firmly shut and there were no entry points. He didn't have the right tools to break in.

He'd have to do things a different way.

He quickly pulled out the SUCTION CREEPERS. Taking one in each hand, he slammed them as hard as he could against the wall of the building. They made a loud sucking noise as they attached themselves to the brickwork.

Moving one hand above the other, Max started rapidly scaling the wall. He pulled himself up on to the flat roof and ducked behind a chimney.

Krusher and Spike were about thirty metres away. Krusher was fiddling with the Activation Pod. Spike was speaking into a mobile phone.

"All is set!" Spike announced to Krusher with delight. "The last Z-Bots will be in children's hands at 7 o'clock on the dot – just as we planned. All systems are GO!"

Max checked his watch: 6.55 p.m. He felt panic rising in his chest. He had to stop Krusher turning thousands of kids into his mindless army! He scurried along the roof towards the robots. But when he was ten metres away, he tripped on an air vent and fell to the ground with a thud.

"IT'S THAT BOY AGAIN!" yelled Spike.

Krusher spun round and his eyes fell on Max. "YOU!" he bellowed. "I thought Metal Meathead finished you off!"

"Sorry, other way round," replied Max.

"Not ... not ... my Meathead," said Spike in a wobbly voice.

"Stop blubbing!" snapped Krusher. "And as for you," he said, turning to Max, "you're too late, FOOL. Very soon we will be inviting all of our friends over here to enjoy OUR RULE! Finally we'll have our revenge on the human race for mistreating robots and using us as their slaves!"

"That's RUBBISH!" shouted Max. "We use robots for science and research, and most of them are treated really well! Anyway, what about you and your drones? Aren't they slaves?"

"What about them!" screamed Krusher.

Suddenly a huge spotlight swept over the rooftop, fixing itself on Max and the robots. There was a gasp from the heaving crowd outside the Coronet and seconds later everyone started rushing in the direction of the rooftop for a better view of the unfolding events.

"What a fantastic stunt!" someone shouted.

"Can you believe they've laid this on for us!" another cried.

"This is better than any film!" hollered another.

Max cursed.

They all think it's part of the show!

Max lunged at the Activation Pod, but Krusher deftly leaped aside and Max fell to the ground.

"OOOOOOH!" gasped the crowd below.

Max struggled to his feet.

"YOU CAN'T DO THIS!" he shouted.

"WE CAN AND WE WILL!" cackled Krusher.

Max prepared to make another lunge at Krusher, but Spike pulled out a large silver laser gun.

"SENSATIONAL!" cheered the crowd.

Max launched himself forward as Spike pressed the trigger.

In a lightning move, Max dived to his left as a red laser bolt shot out of the gun. The bolt flashed past Max, hit a section of chimney behind him and ricocheted straight back.

"AWESOME!" shouted the crowd.

Spike was directly in the line of fire.

The bolt caught Spike full on the chest and sent him flying backwards. He smashed straight into Krusher and they tumbled towards the edge of the roof.

But as he fell, Spike threw out his hand and grabbed Max by the ankles.

Together, all three of them toppled right over the edge of the roof.

MAX FLASH
MISSION 6
CHAPTER 21

"NOOOOOOOOO!" they screamed in unison as they plummeted through the air.

As they hurtled downwards, Max spotted a large striped awning at the front of a restaurant below. Whether it would be strong enough to break their fall was another matter.

They all hit its springy surface and bounced high up into the air.

Max saw his chance. As he shot upwards, he lashed out with his left leg and booted Spike right in the middle of his metal stomach.

The robot screamed and went flying over the edge of the awning. He landed on the cobbled stones with an almighty crash, and smashed into a thousand pieces. The crowd gasped and edged backwards to escape the shards of flying metal.

Max hit the awning a second time and bounced up again. The crowd held its breath as a huge metal fist came smashing towards his face. Max twisted his body into a somersault, missing the punch and sending the robot shooting forwards.

Krusher howled as he plunged off the awning. He hit the ground with tremendous force and shattered into bits.

After a few more bounces, Max came to a stop. He leaned over the side of the awning and spotted the Activation Pod among a huge mess of metal fragments.

He was about to give a sigh of relief when out of the corner of his eye he spotted

Krusher's disembodied hand scuttling over the cobbles towards it.

Max leaped off the awning towards the Pod, rolling over on the ground to break his fall. He scrambled to his feet.

But the hand had got there first. A long metal finger extended and hovered over the silver button.

Max dived forwards, kicking the Pod out of the hand's reach. There was a sickening CRUNCH as he brought his right foot down on the hand with all his might.

Good riddance!

Max bent down and picked up the Activation Pod.

There was an outbreak of thunderous applause from the watching crowd, who by now were standing some way back.

Max looked up at the kids with their Z-Bots. They were not hypnotized. They were not an army. Max had foiled the robots' Great Plan!

But the screeching of tyres suddenly diverted his attention. A black van skidded to a halt a few metres away from him, and two figures wearing balaclavas leaped out.

More robots! No way!

Instinctively, Max began to run, but one of them seized him by the shoulder and threw him into the back of the van. The door slammed shut and he heard the lock click. He tried the handle, but it wouldn't budge. He was trapped. He looked out through a glass panel in the door as the two figures switched on a large, black vacuum-cleaner type object and started sucking up all of the metal fragments.

The crowd burst into applause again. These film-marketing people had thought of everything – even the speedy clean-up operation!

At least Max still had the Activation Pod.

Max thought fast. If these two got hold of it, they'd be able to activate the Z-Bots and all of his work would be for nothing! But he didn't want to try smashing the Pod in case he activated the Z-Bots by accident. In desperation, he tucked it under his sweatshirt.

The van door was yanked open and two huge sacks of metal fragments were tossed into the back. The doors were then slammed shut again. A second later, the engine sprang to life and the van sped out of the square.

Max's body tensed up. Surely it wouldn't be long before they tried to prise the Pod off him? How was he going to get out of this one? But suddenly, the van came to a stop and the panel separating the cab from the back slid open. The two figures whispered something to each other and then slowly peeled off their balaclavas.

To Max's astonishment, they weren't robots at all.

It was his mum and dad.

MISSION 6

CHAPTER 22

"What the...?" gulped Max in utter amazement.
He crawled over to them.

Mum reached her arms through the gap and
gave him a massive hug. "Sorry about the
kidnapping," she said. "Hope you weren't too
freaked out?"

"I'm fine," replied Max, "but what are you
two doing here?"

"Zavonne's team have been monitoring the
warehouse and they tracked you to Leicester
Square," explained Dad.

"They realized there might be some sort of face-off," added Mum. "We were just round the corner at the theatre, so Zavonne sent us in."

"You did brilliantly back there," grinned Dad. "You stopped them just in time."

"Absolutely!" Mum beamed. "Fantastic work!"

"Hang on a sec," said Max. "I thought you two gave up on DFEA stuff years ago."

"So did we." Mum grinned. "But we were hardly going to refuse a job that involved helping our own son out, were we!"

A massive battle with power-crazed robots and a lift home from your parents at the end of the day – could life get any crazier?

"Max," said another voice.

Max turned round and saw the familiar face of Zavonne projected on to the wall of the van.

"A courier will be visiting your home in one hour from now to collect the Activation Pod and what remains of the robots."

"OK," replied Max.

"I take it you used all three gadgets?"

"I did," said Max.

Zavonne pursed her lips.

Come on, Zavonne – praise me for once! I saved the world's kids from turning into evil earth wreckers! Instead they've all just got free Z-Bots to play with!

"The portal in the warehouse leading from our world to theirs has been permanently shut down by our Operatives," said Zavonne. "And the warehouse was burned down in an 'unfortunate' industrial fire, thus leaving no evidence of anything untoward."

"He did well, didn't he?" called Mum from the front of the van.

Zavonne paused and Max held his breath.

"The mission is now complete," said Zavonne flatly.

But as her face disappeared from the screen Max thought he caught her giving him a wink.

"After all your heroics, do you fancy a day out tomorrow?" asked Mum.

"Definitely!" replied Max.

"We could catch a film," said Dad, "how do you fancy REVENGE OF THE KILLER ROBOTS?"

Max groaned as his mum and dad started laughing and the van sped on into the night.

EPILOGUE

In a maximum security DFEA strongroom, Krusher's voice could be heard talking to Spike.

"You see that piece over there?"

"Yes."

"That's one of my fingers."

"No it isn't," replied Spike, "it's one of mine!"

"I can recognize my own finger!" insisted Krusher.

"It's not yours," sulked Spike.

Their disembodied mouths scowled at each other, surrounded by thousands and thousands of their body parts.

"I guess rebuilding ourselves might take a while then," said Spike quietly.

"If we're lucky," replied Krusher sourly.

They were silent for a few seconds more.

"Krusher?" said Spike.

"Yes."

"I've got this itch on my left ear."

"So?"

"You couldn't scratch it with that bit of your jaw could you?"

"No way!"

"Go on."

"No."

"Please?"

Krusher sighed heavily. "All right," he said reluctantly, giving Spike's ear a quick scratch.

"But don't tell anybody."

"Of course not," promised Spike.

"Is that better?"

"Yeah, thanks."

They were silent for another few seconds.

"Hey, Krusher?"

"What is it this time?"

"It's the bottom of my right nostril, you couldn't just...?"

"Forget it," snapped Krusher.

Have you got the rest of my books?

GOT
IT ?

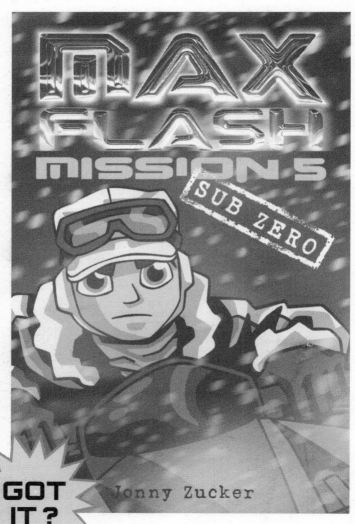

MAX FLASH

MISSION 5

SUB ZERO

GOT
IT ?

Jonny Zucker